BUFFALO WILD!

words by
Deidre Havrelock

pictures by
Azby Whitecalf

annick
press
toronto · berkeley

Translation Note

Kokum is the Plains Cree word for grandmother.

Cover art by Azby Whitecalf, designed by Paul Covello
Edited by Claire Caldwell
Interior designed by Paul Covello

Annick Press Ltd.

We acknowledge the support of the Canada Council for the Arts and the Ontario Arts Council, and the participation of the Government of Canada/la participation du gouvernement du Canada for our publishing activities.

Library and Archives Canada Cataloguing in Publication

Title: Buffalo wild! / words by Deidre Havrelock ; pictures by Azby Whitecalf.
Names: Havrelock, Deidre, author. | Whitecalf, Azby, illustrator.
Identifiers: Canadiana (print) 20210166916 | Canadiana (ebook) 20210166924 | ISBN 9781773215334 (hardcover) | ISBN 9781773215365 (PDF) | ISBN 9781773215358 (HTML)
Classification: LCC PS8615.A8173 B84 2021 | DDC jC813/.6—dc23

Published in the U.S.A. by Annick Press (U.S.) Ltd.
Distributed in Canada by University of Toronto Press.
Distributed in the U.S.A. by Publishers Group West.

Printed in China

annickpress.com
children.deidrehavrelock.com
azbywhitecalf.com

Also available as an e-book.
Please visit annickpress.com/ebooks for more details.

Buffalo had always been part of Declan's life.

When he was born ...

Buffalo belong to the Creator

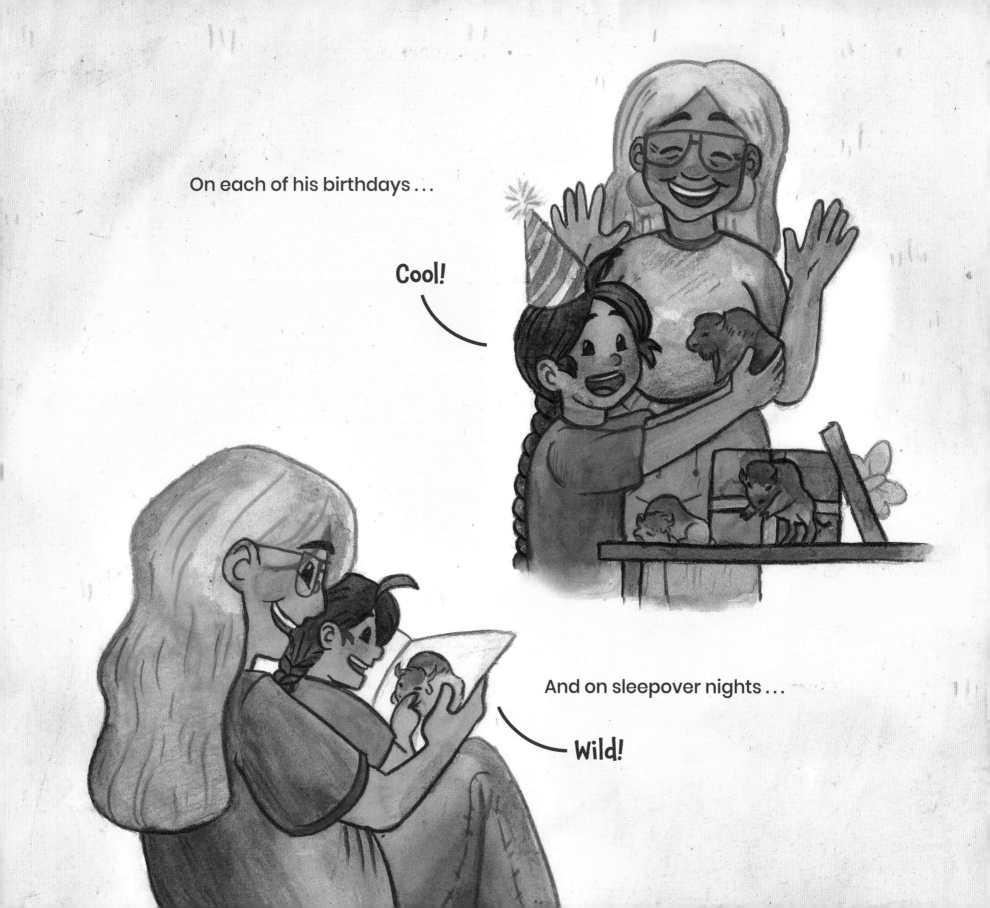

"But Kokum," said Declan one evening. "Where are all the Buffalo?"

"A long time ago, our friends the Buffalo once made this land their home," said Kokum. "We roamed wild and free together, healthy and strong, but now . . . those Buffalo live in the sky."

"Our world will tremble when those Buffalo finally draw near, ready to come home."

"Wow!" said Declan.

That night, Kokum's mysterious
words followed Declan to bed.

"I wish those Buffalo would draw near
and come home," said Declan.
"We belong together."

Outside, the street lights trembled.

Inside, Declan's ceiling began to vibrate.

Could it be?

Across from Kokum's home the prairie
park stood empty, but in the sky . . .

Yes! The Buffalo were there, stampeding across a shimmering field that lay next to the moon—heading for home . . .

Except, a gate of stars held them back.

Declan's heart sank. The Buffalo couldn't come home—not unless . . .

Grabbing his lacrosse stick
and three of his Buffalo sculptures,
Declan headed outside.

He eyed that starry but sturdy gate
and shot a Buffalo into the night.

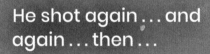

He shot again . . . and
again . . . then . . .

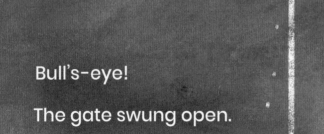

Bull's-eye!

The gate swung open.

Millions of Buffalo were freed.

"Yes! Yes! Come home! Come!" shouted Declan, going absolutely Buffalo wild!

The whole world trembled!

Buffalo filled up the park,
overflowing into the yards nearby.

Wild, wonderful beasts stormed the
lawns, trampling the hedges—including
Kokum's neatly trimmed topiary.

Wild, wonderful beasts stormed the gardens, mashing the flowers—including Kokum's prized chocolate sunflowers.

Wild, wonderful beasts stormed the patios, shattering the gnomes—including Kokum's favorite lawn sculpture.

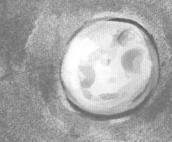

"This land must have been less
crowded a long time ago," said Declan.
"I'll have to send them back."

So Declan pounded his feet. Stern words shot
from his mouth. "Time-out! GO TO YOUR ROOM!"

But Buffalo don't like to be badgered by boys.

Powerful beasts pushed toward Declan,
destroying the fences and sheds—including
Kokum's handcrafted yoga gazebo!

"Help!" cried Declan.

But Kokum didn't hear.

Just then Declan remembered Kokum's words:
"Buffalo belong to the Creator."

"Creator!" called Declan. "Your Buffalo are wild and I want them to stay. But it's Buffalo wild down here. Buffalo wild! In the wildest way!"

Up in the sky, a star twinkled just right. The Buffalo understood.

Millions of heavy-hoofed beasts stormed the heavens,
jolting Kokum from bed.

The Buffalo disappeared across the shimmering field that lay next to the moon.

Without the Buffalo, the prairie didn't seem nearly as wild.

“DECLAN!” called Kokum. “Look! The Buffalo have come home to us!”

Creator had let a few Buffalo stay behind.

And, of course . . .
Declan went wild!

Author's Note

I saw my first Buffalo at Elk Island National Park when I was five years old. This protected wilderness area is just southwest of Saddle Lake Cree Nation, where my family, on my maternal side, originates. Now, it's not difficult to describe how those Buffalo made me feel . . . happy, wild wonderment! Later, while walking through the mall with my dad, I came face-to-face with an adorable crocheted Buffalo for sale at a craftsperson's booth. I immediately pressed him to my chest as though I had found a long-lost friend. That Buffalo, who sat on my bed for years to come, became a constant, rather heartbreaking reminder that these animals who once roamed the land in the millions had faced extinction. Oh, how I wished Buffalo could live in outrageous abundance once again! Much later, when I was in my twenties, my love for this animal took an interesting turn. I started a catering business where I specialized in bison meat. I wanted to reintroduce Indigenous Peoples to their original food source as well as help bison ranchers become sustainable so herds could grow. I even served bison at my own wedding!

These days, I don't eat Buffalo as much as I write (and dream) about them. I wrote this wonderfully wild book to celebrate the return of Buffalo from the edge of extinction and to honor the Buffalo Treaty, a modern-day treaty of cooperation, renewal, and restoration between Buffalo and the First Peoples of North America.

Indigenous Peoples relied on Buffalo for all their needs: food, clothing, shelter, and even spirituality. Because of this, we share a sacred union with Buffalo. This relationship was granted to us by the Creator. Creator is a name many Indigenous Peoples use to address God. In Plains Cree, Creator/God is known as Manitow (ᒪᓂᑐᐤ). Since our loving Creator formed our union with Buffalo specifically for our well-being, our shared journey is not destined to end with heartache and extinction. Rather, I believe our journey leads to an extraordinary time of healing and restoration. Our sacred journey is a celebration of resilience. It speaks of hope, outrageous abundance, thrilling adventure, and reconnection. *Buffalo Wild!* is what my heart sings. I hope yours does, too.

—Deidre Havrelock

A Note on the Buffalo Treaty

In the worldview of First Nations Peoples, relationships are very important. Elders speak about "all my relations" meaning everything in creation: animals, plants, the land, and the sky world. Treaties are about relationships between nations. The signatories of the Buffalo Treaty, through the Treaty, intend to cooperate, renew, and restore the relationship with the Buffalo. The Buffalo, just like a superstar to a sports team, is a keystone animal for the environment and a keystone animal for Indigenous cultures and spirituality. Declan's story brings to mind the Blackfoot word "tsiniksini," which means storytelling. The deep meaning of "tsiniksini" speaks to involvement in an action, in a happening, in an event. Dreams allow us to be "involved" while we sleep. Declan's dream is a wonderful story, the kind of story the signatories of the Buffalo Treaty were dreaming about.

—Amethyst First Rider

For more information visit:
www.buffalotreaty.com

Amethyst First Rider is a member of the Kainai Nation, Blackfoot Confederacy, Alberta, Canada and married to Leroy Little Bear. She is central to the development and success of *The Buffalo: A Treaty of Cooperation, Renewal and Restoration*. Signed by over 30 First Nations and Tribes in Canada and the USA, it is the biggest modern Treaty amongst First Nations. She is also a founding-advisor to the Kainai Ecosystem Protection Association. As a leader in the performing arts community for 20 years, Amethyst has produced and directed plays depicting Indigenous stories and culture, and she co-conceived *Iniskim*, a puppet lantern performance celebrating the reintegration of Bison into Banff National Park.

THE Buffalo: A TREATY OF COOPERATION, RENEWAL AND RESTORATION
2014

RELATIONSHIP TO Buffalo

Since time immemorial, hundreds of generations of the first peoples of the FIRST NATIONS of North America have come and gone since before and after the melting of the glaciers that covered North America. For all those generations Buffalo has been our relative. Buffalo is part of us and WE are part of Buffalo culturally, materially, and spiritually. Our on-going relationship is so close and so embodied in us that Buffalo is the essence of our holistic eco-cultural life-ways.

PURPOSE AND OBJECTIVE OF THE TREATY

To honor, recognize, and revitalize the time immemorial relationship we have with Buffalo, it is the collective intention of WE, the undersigned NATIONS, to welcome Buffalo to once again live among us as CREATOR intended by doing everything within our means so WE and Buffalo will once again live together to nurture each other culturally and spiritually. It is our collective intention to recognize Buffalo as a wild free-ranging animal and as an important part of the ecological system; to provide a safe space and environment across our historic homelands, on both sides of the United States and the Canadian border, so together WE can have our brother, the Buffalo, lead us in nurturing our land, plants and other animals to once again realize THE Buffalo WAYS for our future generations.

PARTIES TO THE TREATY

WE, the undersigned, include but not limited to BLACKFEET NATION, BLOOD TRIBE, SIKSIKA NATION, PIIKANI NATION, THE ASSINIBOINE AND GROS VENTRE TRIBES OF FORT BELNAP INDIAN RESERVATION, THE ASSINIBOINE AND SIOUX TRIBES OF FORT PECK INDIAN RESERVATION, THE SALISH AND KOOTENAI TRIBES OF THE CONFEDERATED SALISH AND KOOTENAI INDIAN RESERVATION,TSUU T'INA NATION along with other nations.

ARTICLE I - CONSERVATION

Recognizing Buffalo as a practitioner of conservation, We, collectively, agree to: perpetuate conservation by respecting the interrelationships between us and 'all our relations' including animals, plants, and mother earth; to perpetuate and continue our spiritual ceremonies, sacred societies, sacred languages,and sacred bundles to perpetuate and practice as a means to embody the thoughts and beliefs of ecological balance.

ARTICLE II - CULTURE

Realizing Buffalo Ways as a foundation of our ways of life, We, collectively, agree to perpetuate all aspects of our respective cultures related to Buffalo including customs, practices, harvesting, beliefs, songs, and ceremonies.

ARTICLE III - ECONOMICS

Recognizing Buffalo as the centerpiece of our traditional and modern economies, We, collectively, agree to perpetuate economic development revolving around Buffalo in an environmentally responsible manner including food, crafts, eco-tourism, and other beneficial by-products arising out of Buffalo's gifts to us.

ARTICLE IV - HEALTH

Taking into consideration all the social and health benefits of Buffalo ecology, We, collectively, agree to perpetuate the health benefits of Buffalo.

ARTICLE V - EDUCATION

Recognizing and continuing to embody all the teachings we have received from Buffalo, We, collectively, agree to develop programs revolving around Buffalo as a means of transferring intergenerational knowledge to the younger and future generations and sharing knowledge amongst our respective NATIONS.

ARTICLE VI - RESEARCH

Realizing that learning is a life-long process, We, collectively, agree to perpetuate knowledge-gathering and knowledge-sharing according to our customs and inherent authorities revolving around Buffalo that do not violate our traditional ethical standards as a means to expand our knowledge base regarding the environment, wildlife, plant life, water, and the role Buffalo played in the history, spiritual, economic, and social life of our NATIONS.

ARTICLE VII - ADHESIONS

North American Tribes and First Nations, and NATIONS, STATES, AND PROVINCES may become signatories to this treaty providing they agree to the terms of this treaty.

ARTICLE VIII - PARTNERSHIPS AND SUPPORTERS

WE, collectively, invited Non-Governmental organizations, Corporations and others o{the business and commercial community, to form partnerships with the signatories to bring about the manifestation of the intent of this treaty. Organizations and Individuals may become signatories to this treaty as partners and supporters providing they perpetuate the spirit and intent of this treaty.

ARTICLE VIII - AMENDMENTS

This treaty may be amended from time-to-time by a simple majority of the signatories.

Deidre Havrelock is a member of the Saddle Lake Cree Nation in Alberta, Canada. She was raised in Edmonton, Alberta with a ghost in her house, a feminist for a grandma, and wishing she had a Buffalo for a pet!

Azby Whitecalf is a Plains Cree illustrator and character designer residing in Saskatchewan. Whitecalf is a graduate of AUArts, majoring in illustration with a bachelor's degree in design. They have fondness for fantasy stories, whimsical tales, and vibrant characters.

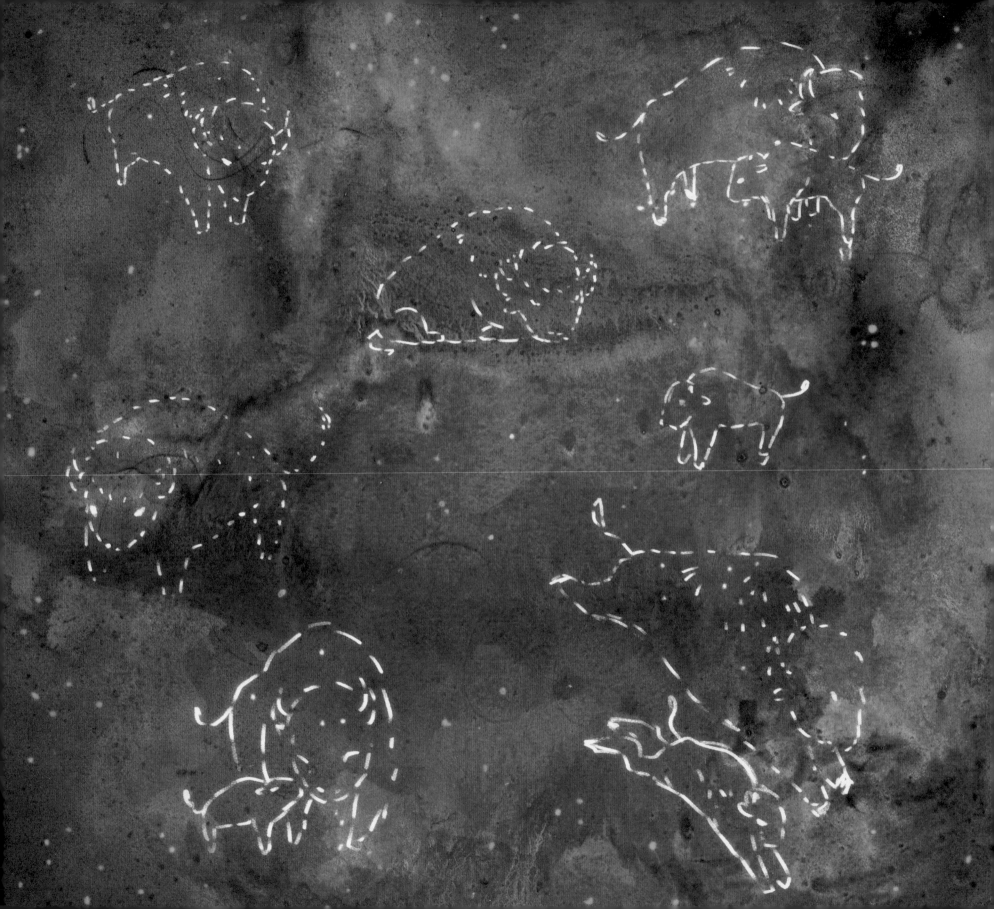